> Dedicated to young
> magic makers everywhere.

Copyright @ 2021 by Payal Gandhi
Library of Congress Number: 2021919059

ISBN: 978-1-7378846-5-1

First printing.
Typeset in Noto Serif SC.
The puzzle pieces and characters in this book were rendered
in digital brush and pencil with finishes in a vibrant vintage palette.

Summary: An imaginative child finds her dreams manifest as she takes
on the challenge of piecing together a magical puzzle.

Subjects: Juvenile Fiction - Imagination & Play; Family/Multigenerational - Grandmothers; Belonging & Identity; Performing Arts/Circus; Animals - Tigers, Cats.

Published by The Organic Study
3729 Sacramento Street
San Francisco, CA 94118

All rights reserved. No part of this publication may be reproduced, stored in a retrieval system, or transmitted in any form or by any means, electronic, mechanical, photocopying, recording, or otherwise, without written permission from the publisher, nor be otherwise circulated in any form other than that in which it is published.

Manufactured responsibly.

10  9  8  7  6  5  4

# MAGIC PUZZLE

by Miss Gandhi

illustrated by Francesca Cosanti

THE ORGANIC STUDY | SAN FRANCISCO, CA

**Ollie was BORED!** She'd counted every curio in Grandma's house. She'd watered every plant. She'd even played with every toy tucked away in the cupboard.

Fancy pillows thrown to the ground barely bounced twice!

Annoyed, she kicked a pickleball ball under the couch.
A soft thud sounded - the ball was stuck.

With her long reach below, Ollie pulled out the ball
and with it **a tattered box.**

"Oh Ollie, you found an old treasure!" Grandma said. "My own grandmother gave that puzzle to me when I was not much older than you. A challenge for sure and **magical** too! It will keep you busy for hours!"

*Magical? Treasure?* Ollie thought. Now that sounded interesting!

Ollie brushed a thin layer of dust from the box. She squinted to make out the picture on top, but it was no use. It was too faded.

*Hmm I see shades of blue and chartreuse; a hint of lilac and a touch of green.*

Ollie continued to wonder.

*Looks like a familiar scene. Could it be where the ocean meets the beach?*

*Well only one way to find out*, Ollie thought. With that, she found a cozy spot and emptied the box.

One by one, Ollie inspected the scattered pieces.

There were exactly 100 in all!

*That doesn't seem so bad*, Ollie thought.
*I wonder why Grandma called it challenging.*

Then, as she did with any puzzle, Ollie began sorting the pieces by color. Arranged borders next and found all four corners too.

Ollie fit the first few pieces together right away. But then she got stuck. **Colors, shapes - nothing seemed to match.**

She was trying to force two indigo colored pieces together when the clock struck eight.

"Ollie, it's bedtime!" Grandma called.

Ollie shook her head, pulling her focus from the puzzle. She couldn't believe how fast time had flown by!

"Just a little longer?" she begged. **"I'm not tired!"**

Grandma peered over from behind Ollie. "You've made great progress," she said. "But you know, this puzzle is very challenging. You'll need all your energy to see it through."

Grandma was right. **It was challenging.** What she didn't understand was why. It was only 100 pieces. Ollie did bigger puzzles all the time!

Bleary-eyed, Ollie gave up struggling.

"Don't worry, Ollie," Grandma continued. "The pieces aren't going anywhere. They'll be right here waiting for you."

That night, **Ollie dreamt in fives.** Animals twirled in a colossal show of five magical acts. A very talented zebra juggled five colorful balls. A mother tiger followed by her four cubs leapt to the stage one by one.

The next morning, Ollie woke up refreshed. She raced back to her cozy spot. "I'm ready to conquer this puzzle once and for all!" she announced.

A few pieces fell right into place. But it wasn't long before she struggled to fit pieces together again. It seemed the puzzle was full of mismatched colors and strange shapes.

## Nothing made sense!

Suddenly, Ollie's leg began to tingle. She'd been sitting in one place for so long that her foot had fallen asleep! Her cozy spot certainly didn't feel cozy anymore.

Ollie stood to shake it off. One leg kicked up and she twirled; then she struck a pose like the grandest circus ringmaster.

"Ugh," she groaned. "I'd much rather play!"

"Patience, Ollie," Grandma said, checking in on her. "That puzzle will require all your focus. Give it your time, and you will see rewards at the end."

Nodding, Ollie stretched her arms and legs, then dove back into the puzzle to find the matching pieces.

But the pieces teased Ollie like a game of charades.

Could it be a swan's crown or a fawn's tail?

An elm tree's ring or a dragon's wing?

A magician's hat or a chimney's cap?

"Wait!" Ollie shouted, sitting up straight.

"THAT is most definitely a rat!"

Ollie tried again and again to push jagged edges against each other, but the pieces just didn't fit. So close, but just not right.

*How will I ever finish this puzzle?*

Frustrated, Ollie got up again. She needed a break!

Ollie stepped up on a stool and reached for her favorite book. A bouncy ball rolled off a high shelf, heading straight towards the ground.

"Oh, no you don't,"
Ollie said, reaching to catch it.
Two more followed.
Balancing on the stool,
Ollie juggled in place.

"Keep trying, Ollie,"
Grandma said as she passed by.
"Stick with it. Sometimes that's
all it takes. Change your
point of view and things
start falling into place."

Ollie looked down at the puzzle.
She rotated her head a bit
and this time noticed the
impressive progress
she'd made.

Back beside the puzzle, one by one she held pieces up high. Squinted to blur her vision a bit in the light.

"It looks like a puppy!" she said. "A dalmatian ready to leap."

"No, it's an orca in its elegant dive."

"A bubble eye goldfish swimming to its grandma's side."

"A great horned owl."

"A cottontail rabbit."

"Little bunny, this one looks like a baleen whale!" she exclaimed.

Animal after animal,
Ollie discovered a new world.

As if by magic, patterns and shapes lined up. Shady fragments grew into shady figures until there was only one piece left.

Then Ollie stalled again. *Where could it possibly be?* she wondered.

This time she couldn't find a trick to distract herself from her frustration.

"This is no fun! After all that work, I can't find the last puzzle piece!!"

"Time for bed!" Grandma said, popping in. "Come on now, Ollie, take a break."

"But I'm not finished!!! How can I give up now?" Ollie cried.

"Fresh start tomorrow. You'll come back with a new angle. That last piece will turn up where you least expect it… I promise," Grandma assured.

That night Ollie's dreams took her back to **the circus.**

This time she found a place in **the magical act.**

The next morning, Ollie marched towards her cozy spot.

*I won't let this puzzle defeat me,* she thought. *But where is that* ***stubborn last piece?***

Then she noticed outlines of the pieces already set in place. Two fit perfectly together like a key to the door. Another two interlocking in a warm embrace.

With fresh excitement, she leapt out of her cozy spot.

And just like that, puzzle pieces leapt up too, then twirled in the air behind her.

To Ollie's delight, with a twirl towards the window and one step on the carpet's edge, she found exactly what she was searching for stuck to her foot.

She reached down to pick up the missing puzzle piece. The piece had a special message on its back.

*Sometimes I just don't fit in.*

Ollie smiled. And just like that...

... puzzle pieces delightfully settled back to the ground. With the last piece placed exactly where it belonged, Ollie marveled at a familiar scene.

"Grandma, I did it!" she called out.

Grandma rushed back to the study from the kitchen. "Amazing, Ollie!" she said. "You're officially a **master puzzle maker!** See how you directed the scene? Did it not turn out just like you imagined?"

Ollie smiled. Indeed, it turned out
**just like her wildest dreams.**

CPSIA information can be obtained
at www.ICGtesting.com
Printed in the USA
BVHW092247281221
625048BV00008B/1758